I
Al

Liz Cashdan

Five Leaves Publications

LAUGHING ALL THE WAY

*Published in 1995 by Five Leaves Publications
PO Box 81, Nottingham NG5 4ER.*

© *Liz Cashdan*

Printed in Great Britain by Antony Rowe
ISBN 0 907123 46 5

For Anna

EAST
MIDLANDS
ARTS

*With financial assistance from
East Midlands Arts*

Some of these poems first appeared in Staple, Anglo-Welsh Review, New Women Poets, Jewish Quarterly, Sheffield Thursday, Northern Poets 2, Lancaster Literature Festival, Poetry from Aberystwyth and Tees Valley Writer.

CONTENTS

PART ONE

The Photograph Box	5
In Memoriam: Uncle Ossia	6
Aunt Regine	7
Uncle Naum	8
Wool Trade	9
Photograph of My Father	10
Laughing All The Way	11
Accents	12
To My Elder Brother	13
A Death	14
The Jewish Girl	15
Passover Incident	16
Horse-writing	17
Our Governess	18
Swarm	19
Caterine	20
Holiday 1934	21
Musical Box	22
The Garden Party	23
Sunday Lunch	24
September 1938	24
On The Bottle	25
The Loggia	26
Fifty Years On	27
Birthday Present	28
Chickens	29
Sent to the Headmistress	30
After School	31
Women Walking	32
Rope Ladder	33
The Cotton Reel Tin	34
The Jewish Wedding	35
Before The Troubles?	36
There's None so Deaf	38
The Lowering of the Watertable	39
Ironies	40
Deconstructions	40
Two Returns	41
Cutting Loose	42

Mixed Singles	42
Scrabble Words	43
Drinking Vodka	44
Festival of Lights	45
Purim Spiel	46
Archaeologies	47
Oral History	49
Concert in Dachau	51
Looking for my Mother	52
Hide and Seek	53
Cote du Nacre	54

PART TWO

Woman Taking Notes	55
Kepler's Women	62
The Tyre-Cairo Letters	66

Glossary	71

The Photograph Box

A smell of deaths and feuds,
faint at first, thickens as I lift the lid:
I shuffle their lives –
uncles, cousins, aunts, jostled and hustled.
I conjure with place-names from the past,
Woolacombe, Karlsbad, Bialystok, Lodz;
jumble the people, hurry them along
to their seaside frolics, army manouevres
and tea on the lawn.

Now in-laws, who bit each other's backs,
rub shoulders, lie side by side
or even face to face.

My fat matriarch, grandmother Fanny,
in brown and fading dress, high bust and bun,
welcomes her sad daughters-in-law
whom once she scolded and reproached.

Benno, for whom my own son Ben is named,
stands proud in his pre-war Polish garden:
I have no spell, no sleight of hand
to free him from his death in Maijdenek.

Now it is their ghosts fumbling my fingers,
I want these photographs back in the box.

Aunt Regine

October 1917
Moscow and revolution:
Uncle Leo and Aunt Regine

take the train to Helsingfors.
Did they pass Lenin's shadow
on the way? Of course

now Leo's in the wool trade
they've left their youth
and politics behind; made

sure that Finland gives
them sanctuary. But Leo hates
sorting oily wool. He lives

for travel and the finer life,
becomes a diplomat; travelling
diplomatically he takes his wife

to Rome where money grows
in groves of twisted olive trees
on the Frascati hills. Then goes

back north leaving Regine
to wealth and loneliness, to spend
her idle days caught between

scolding servants like Angelo
who's made to wear white gloves
at table so as not to show

his chauffeur's dirty finger nails,
and parading her gentility through
marble floors and halls. She fails

to notice how the world outside
has changed. Now frail and grey
she sips Chianti, rheumy-eyed;

while terror of the left and right
grips Italy, and on the Via Veneto
the politicians fight

a losing battle for democracy.
She won't recall her student days.
the plans they made for liberty.

Wine stains the floor-tiles red:
her trembling fingers now betray
an emptiness of heart and head.

In Memorium: Uncle Ossia 1894–1910

Grey wool scratched his skin.
He walked over the grey Moscow square,
hard cobbles pressing his feet,
to the black prison walls.
Ran his hand along the railing,
rusted paintflakes stuck to his damp palm.
He felt the limp paper in his pocket,
creased and recreased it, rolled and rubbed the edges,
scraped the surface with his finger nail
as if illegibility would set him free.
He heard the yard bell ring the prisoners
in from work. He turned,
saw the dull light skid on the river,
then slide into blackness under the bridge.
Behind him, the stamp of feet, the guard's voice,
but he was almost home.

Uncle Naum

I remember Uncle Naum's fat hands:
they made our piano ring like bells,
ring Liszt's Campanilla through the house.

Whatever else he touched just fell apart:
turned down an offer once from lightning zips,
put his money into bottled grape juice,
then watched it ooze away, drop by drop.

When the Germans came to France,
he hid in Vichy till they hauled him off
into a cattle-truck, eastward bound.
He tricked the guards, got back home.

One evening the concierge found him
at the piano, dead.

Wool Trade

Wool was my staple.
For two generations, my grandfather's firm
Elias Trilling and Son, traded raw wool.
Evading pogrom in Bialystok, revolution in Moscow
they travelled and bargained
till Samuel, the son, came to England,
sorting oily bales in dark-roomed offices,
fingering grey wool in dark blue wrappers.
Always tidy in his white clinical coat,
assessing quality, risking orders,
sending telegrams about weights and prices,
he failed with the slump, but regained his losses.

In my silver spoon-fed childhood
words from the wool trade, noil and shoddy,
teased and carded from greasy wool
wove a protecting blanket, warm, patterned,
like the brown rugs from the Bialystok factory.
While on Hampstead's shivering cobbles
rickety kids played backstreet, shoeless
and took our old clothes.

Photograph of My Father

Among the yellowing photographs in the Harrods box
lies one of my father taken on Brighton beach.
His peaked cap, a souvenir from Czarist army days
belies his sixty years and greying hair.
Beside him on the pebbles a youngish girl
looks into his moony eyes and smiles.

Meanwhile my mother and I, on holiday in Buxton
struggle with steps, stairs, indigestion
and inattentive waiters.
My father came to Buxton for the last few days.
Holding his head against his hand,
the tops of his fingers pushed his temple
into folds of skin like shells.

One week later in Barts Hospital he died.
They must have carried him out through the courtyard
past St. Bartholomew the Great, its rounded arches
supporting their aching load eight hundred years,
past Smithfield where the hacked-up meat is sold,
out into the suburbs to the cemetery at Bushey.

Laughing All The Way

Once late at night staying in Menton
I found my father outside the bedroom door
at the Hotel des Anglais
swapping the paired shoes along the corridor.
I couldn't sleep that night. What if
the bootboy challenged me?
Next day we walked the dusty road to Castellar.
At every garden door he rang the bell
a challenge to the villa-owning "Chiens Mechants"
half hidden in the trail of bougainvillea.
I wanted to run but he held my hand,
deliberately slowed his pace.
Back home he played on my fear of dogs
shouting from the top of Hampstead Heath
his voice echoing to St. Pauls, the Surrey hills,
"Help, this dachshund's after me."
He always sliced fruit cake horizontally
taking the topmost nut-packed slice;
made Mother's most-to-be-revered guests blush
with "Would you fancy some of the tarts we're keeping for
tomorrow?"
And after every evening meal
informed my mother categorically
that for once he'd not be helping with the washing up.
She'd fallen for him when still at school,
he'd woo'ed her, urging his Great Dane,
"Go for her," he'd said. She'd gone for him.
I was away at college when he died.
I wonder if he laughed to hear the final diagnosis
turn upset stomach into heart attack.

Accents

I never heard my Mother's foreignness,
only her harsh voice calling my name.
Rough-skinned hands smelling of onion
washed me, combed my hair,
sometimes slapped my legs.
She wouldn't come to school events
frightened of other parents
who'd recognise her Russian consonants.
She stayed at home washing floors,
doing her best with wartime rations,
laughing at Tommy Handley, Monday Night at Eight.

One evening late home from school
(I'd spent two hours corner-talking
while leafy Bucks flattened my Hampstead vowels)
I found her slumped in her dressing-gown
listening to Kreisler on the wireless
Tchaikovsky's violin concerto
crying into her silence.

To My Elder Brother

You threw me over your shoulder
I hated it, hated the upside-down feeling
out of control, in your power.
You laughed and your bald head shone.
Once absent-minded, you drank the tea slops
Mother had poured into your cup.
But you didn't notice, you were locked
into Ximenes, Turkish grammar, Urdu poetry.
For years you worked for Father
selling wool but hating it.
Every night when I went to sleep
you played Chopin, Brahms,
Mozart piano duets all on your own.
You called me little Schwester,
I stuck my long chin out awkwardly towards yours.
I cut my holiday short for your wedding
then watched your wife and Mother
squabbling for love and money.
You had been an old-maid man so many years
we laughed when you called your son
across the garden, "Mat, come to Uncle!"
Then deafness and a slouching gait
led into old age.
"Gout!" the doctor diagnosed your swollen toes.
"Off with his leg," the surgeon said
but the gangrene had crept too far.
So Jack, you were dead.
In the crematorium your little Schwester
saw your coffin slide smoothly
into its secret place.

A Death: Manchester

"I wish I were dead," you used to say
so often when things went wrong.

Now you lie there, ask about what you'll do
when you get better, though you know
and I know that it's out of the question.

And it's too late for all the questions
I should have asked you.

The nurse says "Come and see her, she's nice now."
But I can't go into her room again,
not openly.

I peep when no-one's there,
see a white sheet sculpted
by your toes, knees, face,
like something from a museum.

The Jewish Girl

Let us pray.
The girls flop to the floor
serge tunics flapping the wooden boards.
My toes bend back uncomfortably.
I listen but God has got himself
into the company of Jesus and the Holy Ghost.
I carry the sin in my bent knees
for years.

Passover Incident

"There ye are, Ma'am," the fishmonger said
"the 'ake, the 'addock, the 'alibut and the 'eads."
The fish oozed juices as he wrapped it up.
Back home my mother chopped and fried,
stacked boxes of unleavened bread,
grated horseraddish and bitter herbs.
I polished the wine glasses, set one
for the Prophet Elijah in case he should
be thirsty. How else could the promise
of "next year in Jerusalem" come true?
Then practised the questions I'd learnt by heart:
"Ma nish-tanah ha lie-lah ha-zay?"
twisted my tongue round the Hebrew —
archaic words to sort out the ritual that
made this night different from all other nights.
A retelling of the exodus from Egypt —
we counted the plagues
spilled a drop of wine for each
to show our sorrow for our enemies.
Moses' rod had parted the waters for us
while they drowned in the Red Sea.
"Open the door for Elijah," my father said.
I ran obediently, froze on the doormat
as the letter box flapped and Elijah's hand
dropped the evening post at my feet.

Horse-writing

At the schoolroom table I sit
upright, legs swinging loose.
My father guides the clenched pencil
outlining the Hebrew letters:
samech, vav, samech. The eyes of the *samech*
look back at me from the scrawled lines
Soos, soos, soos, trots across the page
line after line until my hand aches.

Later, my father shows me how to ride
cups his hands so I can swing up
to the high-slung saddle. I sit upright
knees clenched to the leather, elbows close.
"Soos, soos, soos," I urge, dig my heels in.
I look back at my father shielding his eyes
the horse gallops across the field away
from him. I have to hang on tight.

Our Governess

Our governess, Miss Goodbody,
a mucky mawther from St. Germans
was reared on a farm near Sandringham.
The man she might have married died
at Gallipoli. So like a Norfolk turkey
she took our love and gobbled it.

She found us comfortable corners,
cushioned us when mother made us cry.
Her name became a meaning in our lives,
and we, changelings, in our own hearth.

Later, when I was old enough to love them both,
I knew the pain my mother felt in Goody's greed,
winced when she piled her toast with marmalade.
I understood what mother could not understand:
Miss Gimel, as my father nicknamed her, really
did enjoy her food, baked for us all.

Swarm

First there was only the apple tree
and white socks, little white socks
and a pen that wouldn't be controlled;
gardener mowing the lawn above stone steps
where the water tap trickled
and the can was too heavy to lift.
In the corner a square stone of water
but no frogs, only lily of the valley white
from the first of May till June.
But today was the garden party —
the smell of baking from the big kitchen,
Mother up early in a silk kimono
ordering the household.

And then the bees came just before lunch.
First one or two and no sound —
till the sky blackened into a dome
of apple leaf and bee fuzz,
mower silenced by bee-drone.
The garden was a dark world
and we fled indoors.
A cry went up to shut out the bees
and the house was full of people
hurrying to telephone, to counsel war.
And when the guests arrived
they filled the bay window, looked out
to where the cluster of bee grapes hung
on their queen.
Then a spaceman years before space
climbed his ladder into the apple tree
and the bees swarmed into his bee box.

Caterine

Smell of gas and supper cooking
my kitchen, orange, clean,
but while I'm stirring, looking

into the swirl of onion soup
Caterine comes slowly slippered
shuffling and smiling, the droop

of her shoulders in baggy smock.
"I remember you." I frown
in Menton's winter sun, the shock

of January warmth, date palm,
bougainvillea purpling the wall,
mimosa's yellow foam.

Her husband, "the man from Caterine"
in Grandma's faulty English,
digs the dry soil between

the cracking flags, mends pipes
that hiss and grumble in the cellar
depths; he stops and wipes

his forehead with his wasted arm.
I look at her, try French:
"J'ai pas de larmes,

pourquoi vous etes venue?"
"Porkoy," she says in patois
Italian accent ringing through

"porkoy." She stops and grins.
She stirs the huge black pot.
I have to guess at what she means:

the rotten life, the basement flat
a bed of quilts and rags.
"I'm sorry, Caterine, je le regrette."

Those hot days along the prom,
Casino teas, the bandstand,
the glace'ed fruits we bought from

Jean's Confiserie, wrapped, ribboned
laid in wicker basket trays,
treasured, guarded, opened

till teeth cracked the sugared ice,
sank into luscious jelly fruit,
tongue drew and sucked the juice.

Chewing bread and salty cheese
toothless Caterine and her man
mutter their blessings and their curse.

I give the soup a vicious stir.
Caterine, her man are swallowed in the steam.
Slivers of white onion surface in the blur.

Holiday: 1934

Regine, Lili, Vivi, Chou,
our French cousins come to stay
in California, on the Norfolk cliffs.
We wind the handle on His Master's Voice:
Wheezy Anna, Smoke Gets in your Eyes,
You're Lovely to Look at, My Friend Elisabeth.

Smell last year's sun trapped in the bookcase,
drink soft rain water from the moss-edged butt,
never wash, although we swear we have;
feed lettuce to the twitch-nosed rabbit,
lean over fences like gentlemen farmers,
poke the pigs' bristling backs;
ride in Old Tom's Elsan cart
hear him curse Londoners, foreigners.

Across the field beyond the ring of bungalows
cliffs trickle dry sand on to the beach.
We laugh when the huge waves catch us, unaware.

Music Box

"Alle Voglein sind schön da," the birds chirrup,
a strange tobacco smell rises with the tune.
The doorbell rings. It's the cigarette woman,
Mrs Liverman. Her dyed, yellow tobacco hair
hangs stringily round her wrinkled face.

"A witch, a witch," I cry, run to the kitchen,
hide in the chauffeur's pantry with its pile
of bulbs and shoe-black tins. No chauffeur,
business is bad, Mother walks to the shops.

Mrs Liverman has walked these streets year
after year, hung on to the tortoiseshell handles
of her red crochet bag full of eastern Abdullas.
The front door clicks. I sneak back to the music
box, its cigarettes newly stacked, aroma fresh.

I lift the box, struggle to wind the key,
stand back and listen: a whirring of wings,
a small metallic warble, the birds rise and
fall again, a slow going out of tune.

The Garden Party

Before the garden party guests arrived
Pierre took me to the strawberry beds,
pulled me up the slope,
green plants under old tennis nets.
"We're going to Palestine," he said.
We climbed ashore at Acre by the fort,
a string of sullen camels ambled by.
We heard the clang of Turkish scimitars.
He dragged me off the path
treading white flowers into damp clay.
A donkey took us to Jerusalem. Far off
a voice called Pierre to meet the guests:
he left me by the wailing wall alone,
grey brick crumbling in London soot.

Sunday Lunch

Mr Wolf never brings his wife
but I know he has one: Mother
always says: "How is Irenochka?"
Father says: "Kushai makoffku."

I watch Mr Wolf wipe the gravy
off his moustache, blink his eyes.
Father says: "Kushai, Popski, kushai."
The meat is all gristle and fat.

Mr Wolf seems to have no problem
though Mother asks: "How bad is it?"
Mr Wolf says: "The breast has to come off."
The sinews catch my teeth.

"Poor Irenochka," says Mother.
Mr Wolf is swabbing his plate
shiny clean. My gravy has grown
skin. My mouth won't empty itself.

Kushai makoffku is Russian for: Eat your carrots.

September 1938

Evacuated to Tintagel, we walk the wet cliffs, snivel
in damp billets, learn our lessons in the village hall.
Watch the tin-coloured Atlantic beat into the icy caves,
hear it thunder where the sea-thrift blows in the wind,
try to recapture the glory of King Arthur and his Knights
who fell in honourable battle for their lord.

Then Chamberlain comes, smiling, from Munich:
a miracle worked by Merlin's magic, locked
for so long in Cornwall's granite. We take
the long train back to London, ordinary school,
forget about Czechoslovakia.

On The Bottle

I walk between the tourers and the statics
Mediterranean names mocking grey Tintagel sky:
Napoli, Sorrento, Valencia.
Cliff Farm sold out for profit,
neat caravans stacked on mower-trimmed grass,
no tough sheep mouths cropping here.
At the village store I question Mrs Brown
take her back to 1938
Munich and the evacuees.

I was one of the little Londoners
in maroon blazer, wind blowing into
the gap between knickers and lisle stockings.
In the barn with Madge and Helga,
warm, steamy, smelling of cat piss.
Secrets time. Madge knows all about
why Miss Edwards' nose is red.
'She's on the bottle,' says Madge.
I nod wisely, shift on the prickly straw.

'I remember your Miss Edwards,' says Mrs Brown,
'on the bottle, she was, kept it in the sideboard,
thought I didn't know.'

Over Bossinny Cove, witch-like,
Miss Edwards flies astride her bottle,
red nose pointing south,
hiccoughing like the coastguards' helicopter.

The Loggia

September 1939, summer holiday over
we arrive at the new house.
"There's a loggia at the back," my father says.
We've not had one before.
I imagine him squatting in the yard
begging for scraps at the door
peering at the window with watery eyes.
Perhaps he'll come round the front
help us with our luggage
down the long lavender path.
But no-one lets us in.
My hand grips the stair-rail while
a voice from the wireless declares war.
All afternoon we unpack belongings
round the house; emergency rations
in the garden shelter. That's where he'll sleep,
I think, and shudder when my father
clicks the lock.
After tea my sisters pin blankets
over windows to protect the dark.
I wonder if he has a gas mask.
Please God, if there's an air raid
make them let the lodger in.

Fifty Years On

*God give us bases to guard or beleaguer
games to play out whether earnest or fun
fights for the fearless and goals for the eager
twenty and thirty and forty years on.*

School song 1939

Another playground:
she stands in the September sun,
sky netted in the black wire
above colliding circles of white.
"Attack. Shoot, go on, shoot."
The perimeter fence slants its shadows
in front of her.
Church bells ring in the valley.
Invasion or victory?
Birdsong drips into the afternoon
drowns the bounce of the ball.
"Where's the defence? You're not marking."
A whistle tells her it's all over.
Earnest or fun, the game's played out.

Birthday Present

"Is it really necessary?" you say,
not wanting to let me travel all those
wartime miles, High Wycombe to Cheshire

for a youth camp, harvest for victory.
We stook corn with its scratch of skin,
the boys earning 1/9 to the girls' 1/6

though, of course, we work harder.
On the way home in Chester, I buy
you Bach's Toccata and Fugue in D minor,

organ of Christchurch, Oxford, with
His Master's Voice gold and red label,
a shiny black record, safe I hope,

in its ersatz card case. I stow it
on the luggage rack, watch so that
noone will break it, my present to you.

Once I'm back home, you stare at me,
ask when I last washed, say:
"Hurry, supper's ready, we'll talk later."

You take the record, don't look at it,
put it on the chair beneath the window,
bring the warmed-up meal for us to eat.

Then, "Blackout time," you say.
I go to draw the curtains, hear
the black crack of Bach under my knee.

Chickens

Father built the chicken hut:
slats of wood, sawmill-fresh
battened to thin ribs with tiny nails,
deep creosote sinking into wood and lungs.

Now we throw down scratchy yellow straw,
are choked by the powdered chaff.
The hens arrive, cluck and coo, strew
brown feathers on purple lavender,

purple catmint, that finger-crushed
bring echo-smells of long-shut cupboards,
Grandma's tea. Sent to look for eggs,
we hold our breath against the stench

of chicken shit, carry the warm offerings,
lay them in ising glass. Then retch when
Mother stirs the chicken feed, mixes it
with boiling cabbage and potato peel.

Sent To The Headmistress

I knock on the dark green paint
loud because I have no fear
of old Miss Dessin; her giant

feet protrude from her long dark dress
huge hands rest on her lap.
Bubbling with anger I won't confess

to schoolgirl misbehaviour.
"How dare you knock so loud?"
thick glasses magnify her glare.

"You're not a kitchen maid,
I'm not the cook. What is it then?"
Her flabby face congeals, staid.

The room is heavy with her sweaty smell.
They must have bought a special
armchair for her bulk; a swell

of green and yellow beads rattle
on her breast. She beckons me.
I hesitate, anticipating battle,

then hold my paper to her face.
"Miss Herbert said I had to come.
She said we had to trace

repeating patterns for a biscuit tin,
but I'm no good at things like that —"
she takes the paper, drops it in the bin.

Her face is solid, still no smile.
"Well, that makes two of us who cannot draw."
My thoughts are jangled by the half-time bell.

I can't believe she's on my side
so offer her apologies.
"I tried for hours, I really tried."

But now her whole green mound
begins to shake with laughter.
At first a little gurgling sound

until her heaving, roaring torrent
fills the room. It's worse by far
than any schoolroom punishment.

After School

Slowly up the cemetery steps
past white marble and sad mottoes
we climb reluctant home.
A hot day, limp cotton dresses
stuck to sweating bodies. Huge girls
in uniform, absurdly bulging.
Ginnie's secrets fall from her fat lips.
"Laureen," she says, "I stroked her hair
in Maths today." We stare.
Horror widens our eyes.
Muscles tighten in secret places
and still we cannot speak.
Our own silence and the hot afternoon
oppress us. We long to touch
and know we are forbidden.
"Her hand on my arm," says Ginnie,
"I could smell her body."
Ginnie's hand, puffy pink fingers
still swollen from winter chilblains
moving through Laureen's corn-ripe hair.
We stand and stand but Ginnie says no more.
She yawns, elbows us to break the spell.
"Come on," she says, "I want my tea.
It's strawberries today."

Women Walking

Leaving the town settled in its valley
the rattling bus take us to Fingest.
Soon we will walk the Ickneild Way
scuffing cloud-white chalk on brown

schoolgirl shoes. I follow
my older sister and her friend through the summer
glow of beeches, brushing past nettles
their acrid smell, the itch on my arm.

I watch Ruth, her friend Irene, stoop over
wild raspberries, drop the fruit into
white bags which ooze with the red stain.
I hesitate, then join them, fill my mouth,

revelling in the sour sweetness,
the excitement of that first blood
with its smell of growing up that
has allowed me to walk with women.

Rope Ladder
(For Jill)

The rope ladder is your idea.
Your fingers move deftly, knot
the rope round the wooden rungs.

I hear your unsettled breathing
impatient grunts, the crunch of leaves
and a lorry down the valley

revving its engine through the woods
through the beech branches coming
fast into their green blur above.

"Hold on!" you shout, "don't let go."
And I hold on to the rope
pretending the burn on my hands

is nothing; pretending I love
all this rope ladder business;
because you know poetry,

have bewitched me with Ruth Pitter's
"Edam the moon"; have bidden me
"Come Hither" with Walter de la Mare;

lost me in the magic of Dr. Faustus;
but I can't get my balance
on the swing of the rope.

Today, I read in the paper of
your death, feel my foot slip
again on the first rung.

The Cotton Reel Tin: 1981

Jet-stream threads trail over the edge:
Lyons Dundee Cake, in rubbed gold letters.
Spools of Apple Green, Cherry Flair fill
the tin now.

I never did like fruit cake.
Sunday tea in the sitting room,
blue velvet curtains drawn close,
red cherries stuck in my teeth.
Then came the war, no more Dundee.
From Thoroughgoods, the local baker
we bought dry, eggless cakes, hardly
any fruit at all.

That empty crumbliness accompanied
the six o'clock news: " — bombed
the docks at Bremershafen — " a crumb
could choke you: "Seventy-two of our
planes are missing."

Now as I choose my thread I hear
the six o'clock news:
"Forty pilots from World War Two
will meet tonight in Paris to reminisce,
ten British, ten French, ten German."

I say, wizard prang, old chap, you only
just missed shooting me down. Holes in
me plane? Just like plums in a fruit cake!
I finish sewing, drop the cotton reels,
strafe the tin.

The Jewish Wedding

Let us marry this girl in the blue and red
shot taffeta to the young man in the black
suit and Antony Eden hat.
The synagogue is full of his relations.
She stands under the canopy, looks at her shoes
taffeta like her dress: her freesias droop.
His uncle who is a rabbi says things in Aramaic.
She says nothing, makes no promises
but there is a wedding ring on her finger
and she has signed a register —
she must presume herself married, still unclean.
It was a lie when she told his parents
she'd been to the ritual bath.

Here comes the bride, thrilled and terrified
Mendelssohn sings inside her head.
Across the aisle she glimpses
her non-Jewish friends
one of them has forgotten to bring a hat
wears a handkerchief on his head.
There are more jokes to come.

Before the Troubles?

Belfast is *"Up with King Billy", "Down with the Pope"*
shining through the fog from Nutts Corner to city centre;
police with pistols demanding your licence; and on Sunday
the swings are chained in the parks though Ian Paisley's
not been heard of yet. There's the Linen Hall and the biggest
Town Hall in Europe. The moon's up over Harland and Wolf and
there's a man walking on it just like you walk up Antrim Road.

Winter sun blinds as you drive to school along Bangor Road
and you've taken an oath before a J.P. not to upset the
Queen's government in Northern Ireland, as if you would!
"Catholics pay to get into Heaven, don't they, Miss?"
That's Jennifer who failed the Quali (sort of 11-plus)
but her Mum pays for her grammar school place. And because
you're Jewish they ask if you were born in Egypt.

First time living north of London, you're invited out
to supper, but they've had their tea at six o'clock so
all you get is a sandwich and a cuppa well past nine.
It would have been ignorant to ask. They're Protestants,
"And are you a Protestant Jew or a Catholic Jew?" they ask.
Simple answer to that one: orthodox Jews are Protestant.
But when it comes to the Intifada, you know you'll be Catholic.

On Friday night at the Rabbi's, his wife lights candles,
he makes Kiddush, cuts the Challah, doesn't wink but says:
"They didn't teach you to make bread at University, did they?"
No answer, just a mental note that you'll never make bread,
and a promise never to be a good little wife. You work out
a route to town on Saturday that doesn't go past the synagogue
and buy your fillet steak well away from the Antrim Road.

Saturday lunch and your husband's walked the six miles to
the synagogue and back so now it's time for the secret drive
in the sit-up-and beg Ford: cable brakes need pulling up
every two weeks. You're teaching him to drive test-free:
"Give her a wee taste of the petrol," you say as instructor.
He's speeding under Cave Hill away north to Greenisland:
"Drive gormly through Glenslowly," you read the sign to him.

You learn the language fast: bus fare to town is "fippence"
and the kids "want out" but will "fetch something in" to you.
And what they've seen at the cinema is a really good "filum".
Mr Hughes who's converted the flats is wanted by the police.
Is it for connecting the gas to the water or because the flat
upstairs has different occupants every night: you see them
leave when you're having breakfast, still in evening dress.

The place is damp, the trunk under the bed growing mould
and the washing won't dry. On fine days you can climb
Cave Hill, look east along Belfast Lough or west to the
midge-clouds of Lough Neagh, south to the Mountains of Mourne,
but often the mist stops you seeing clear, so when it's
time to pack, take the ferry Larne to Stranraer you won't
find it hard to shake Ulster's Red Hand, say "G'bye now."

There's None so Deaf

All night the waterfall
with its open mouth
in darkness drenches
the slow-moving hours.
Far more insidious than
the dripping of a tap.
The rake of water
pours into the hollow
crevices flooding and
drowning sleep. Daylight
might absorb the sound
but in the dark the
silence will not come.

For you who only think of touching,
the ritual of washing is enough:
you do not hear the waterfall.

The Lowering of the Watertable
Cheshire 1963

From Bollington to Pott Shrigley
the canal's dark in the woods.
She's dragged you here into Sunday's
grey space between the bright tips
of Saturday night and Monday morning.

So now you slouch along the tow path,
slurp through mud, overgrown grasses,
nettles. She tells you about the book
she's been reading, how they've drained
the wetlands so there's more water

for crops and factories.
She tries to make sense of it,
says now the water's too rich in nutrients,
has withered the marsh orchids,
the sedges. "And no birds sing,"

you tease. She stands on the bridge
where the canal joins the river's
turmoil, watches the last shards of
broken light skid on the water's
surface. You want to be home and dry.

Ironies

She used to watch him at the ironing board
proud of his prowess in the tug of war
between his new-learned skill
and the ebb and flow of shirt.
She'd hear the steamer hiss
across recalcitrant waves of silk.
Bravely he'd guide the silver prow
determined on its head-strong course.

Now as they argue over every rucked-up
detail of their lives
she sees him falter and begin to doubt —
realises he's ironed the creases in
not out.

Deconstructions

My hammer will topple a small statue
Nimrod, Nero, Stalin
the name is irrelevant.
A little chisel for chipping at walls
China, Jericho, Berlin
it doesn't matter where
stones come tumbling
down in a dry dribble
of sound.
I will no longer
use my bellows
to puff up the complacent bellies
of little men
who think they're god.

But through the gaps in the wall
come other little men
with swollen heads.

Two Returns

I want to take you back:

the train steams west from
Marylebone Station under
Harrow Road viaducts —
London brick smoked black —
through ribbon suburbs
Uxbridge, Ruislip, Denham
till it snorts into the first
cuttings, white chalk padded
with yellow primroses and then
the beechwoods of Gerrards Cross
and Beaconsfield. I say: "Look!
Loudwater, I played tennis there.
Flackwell Heath, that's where I won
the slow-horse race." I could never
make mine do more than a trot.
The train brakes for High Wycombe.

The ticket collector used to wait
for those green torn-off halves:
they had to be pulled apart
the return bit kept safe for
the journey home.

Now return tickets are thin
slips of paper that have nothing
to do with each other. The day is spent
without making any discoveries.
All I have is your silence
and these flowers I've picked
lying dead on the seat
long before the journey's over.

Cutting Loose

Cutouts today, her mother said,
showing her how to manoevre finger and thumb.
She remembers those nursery days
blunt-ended scissors refusing to turn
neat corners, leaving white half moons
like unexpected halos.
Sometimes the wilful blades would chop off limbs,
slit faces in their clumsy surgery.

Now as she sorts and cuts the photographs
her bungling anger leaves his severed arm
still guiding hers towards their wedding cake.
And when she has to face the family groups
he's so hemmed in, the others suffer
lacerations she only meant for him.

Mixed Singles

(from Durer's engraving of Adam and Eve)

Eve has been wrong-footed
confined in her less-than-half the picture,
crook'd arm mirroring the serpent's
body slither, an apple held
in the fingers of her snake-head hand.
Adam is all male muscle,
his open palm innocent, expectant.
Eve has another apple for him
in her left hand, arm curled
sinistrously behind her back.

We know who will win:
however Eve serves
the linesman calls fault.

Scrabble Words

(in memory of Yitta Cashdan)

On holiday, I'm writing cards
to ancient friends and lonely aunts:
Hilda, eighty, in Addiscombe,
and Dora, I missed her ninetieth
down in Hove.
I nearly addressed one to you.

Last time I visited we played scrabble
your arthritic fingers found it hard
to place the squares, your easy words
made only little scores.
I'd come with a new Visitors' Book
the old one scribbled with two-years worth
of family and friends.

You used to come to stay up north —
I drove you into the White Peak
and the Dark, dug heather stealthily
beside the Derwent reservoir: it grew
like purple fire in N.W.4.
The greenness of your fingers
made avocadoes split their sides
take root, shoot leaves on to your
windowsill; made lemon pips open
their foliage like magic toys from China.

Now there's no more visiting
last entry Sunday May 10th, 1992.
And one card less to send.

Drinking Vodka

Relax, says Tom, *breathe in and hold the breath.*

She watches her son in his jeans tight over the crotch.

Down the vodka in one, he says.
Do not hold the breath.

She isn't sure if she can
but Tom's face is smiling.
She lets the stuff burn her throat.
Tom's girl-friend Nadia having a baby.

Exhale slowly, says Tom.

She likes Nadia. Tom was at the birth,
held Nadia's legs.

It's a complex and wonderful sensation, says Tom.

She smiles for Nadia, for the unknown child,
for Tom who is not the father.

You'll soon get the knack of it, says Tom.

Tom's words are taken from *The Cooking of Russia* by Karen Craig & Seva Novgorodsev.

Festival of Lights

Hurry, it's Chanucah," I shout
wondering why we bother.
"Dad's lighting the first candle."
The two kids, more interested in telly
homework, and whether December's snow
will last through Christmas
come reluctantly to watch.
My fingers smell of Brasso, black under the nails,
the candlestick glows in the lamplight.
A match flares, I catch the tang
connected more to rituals of pipe
than candlestick. The shamash is lit,
a prayer mumbled, giggles suppressed.
The first candle shines — oil for one night only —
the other seven dark, with white wicks
(Woolworth colours for Christmas trees).
Out of tune we sing in remembered Hebrew
"Ma-oz-tzur ye-shou-a-ti" —
the kids, teasing, cut in with
"the cat's in the cupboard and you can't catch me."
Their joke is truer than they know:
Judas Maccabeus saved the Jews
when the Greeks attacked.
Bored with the singing whose words we haven't
let them understand, they hold out hands.
"C'mon, Dad," says Ben eager for the pay-off,
"don't be mean, think of the miracle,
after all we don't get Christmas presents."
"Fuck Chanucah," my daughter says,
"you're both so bloody hypocritical."
The candle gutters in the draught
of the slammed door.

Purim Spiel

Alone in the attic rummaging through boxes
I find Grandmother's dressing-gown
pink velvet edged with pink fluff.
Downstairs a voice on the radio's
killing people in Jerusalem and Gaza.
The pink velvet feels nice and soft.

Funny I can't remember Grandmother in it,
only my children dressing up, fighting
for a royal cloak. Voices in an empty room.
Ahasuerus, King of Babylon, aloof
leaves Haman to organise the masssacres
Esther in pink velvet pleads with him.
I'm in the kitchen rolling dough
filling the Hamantaschen with poppy seed
blue-black, sweet, sticky
ready to celebrate Haman's death.
But the children's voices are ripping
the velvet.

I slide into the dressing gown,
the pink shreds tickle the back
of my nose, the back of my knees.
There is no-one to plead with.
I go downstairs, bin the dressing-gown,
switch off the voices.

Archaeologies

1. BBC News, Beirut 1982

"The rubble must be dug to find the bodies"
Fractured buildings open up,
reveal a broken anatomy.

The mind, held hostage like the town,
is cut apart, dug over.
poked, scraped, sifted.
Finds must be cleaned, catalogued,
numbered, weighed.

2. Masada 1971

We climb, soft-sandalled, up the Roman ramp
unsettling desert dust blown
through Moad's misty sunrise.
On top, a tourist's sun scorches
the burning rock. Jews lived here once.
Now they have dug to find the past:
ovens for bread, ritual baths,
wine jars, cool water wells.

Unable to accept what Rome's machinery of war
forces on the imagination, we find
our entertainment in patched mosaics,
take smiling photographs of friends
in Herod's broken palace.

3. Jerusalem 1983

Leaving Tel Aviv the bus clears
the anytown suburbs, cuts through
cotton fields until the slow climb
into Jerusalem. Here the new pines
die from carbon exhaust, burnt-out
tanks litter the roadside, reviving
older memories, histories from other
lands, uprooted, polished clean,
to be restructured, delicately glued,
stored in museums of the mind.

The Holocaust Museum: tourists wait...
Inside, it is all gloom:
an everlasting light flickers.
Outside, the sunlight is unbearable.

Oral History

1. How Do You Say

Today I am talking Russian and Hebrew.
I am in Tel Aviv, the sun is hot.

Galina has come to clean my sister's house.
In Russia she was a school-teacher.
She recites Pushkin: "It may be that love
has not completely died in my soul."
Once she lived near Chernobyl:
her son Alex may have leukaemia.
Such possibilities are difficult in any language.

On T.V. four hundred Palestinians turn to Mecca,
their faces touch the snow of no-man's-land.
How do you say that in Hebrew?
Jews know the word for exile in every language.
The Palestinians pray in Arabic.

"I am afraid of Arabs," Galina says.
Yesterday the Arab who had come to empty
her dustbin stopped to greet her.
"He would kill me," Galina says.
She uses the conditional particle.
"He would kill to save his children."

Dyeti, yeladot — Russian and Hebrew words.
How do you say children in Arabic?

Oral History

2. Acre Jail

It's January. Avital drives me
from Haifa to Acre. Her grandfather
on the back seat hums a song
to the rain beating across
the Mediterranean on winds
I've seen blow like this
only in northern winters.
This is a Crusader Castle.

He pays at the museum door,
we climb the heritage stairs:
on the wall a young man's face
labelled by the Mandate: illegal
immigrant, terrorist.
Beside me the old man telling the story:
"Yes, we got out of Lithuania, away from
the Nazis, down to Turkey, got a ship,
Istanbul it was, 1942 must have been.
Then just off Haifa we took
the captain, put him in his cabin
and there he stayed while we piloted
the ship, got everyone ashore."

The old man's eyes are steady.
"Arrested me for possession of arms," he says,
"they hanged twelve of my comrades here.
Exiled me to North Africa. I missed
the storming of the jail."

Avital helps him down the layered stones
down to the cells, the place of execution.
The rope hangs over the trapdoor loose.

"How does it feel, coming back?" I ask.
"It's history," he says. "my history."

Concert in Dachau

I thought twice about coming here
to the castle on top of the hill
gardens rich with agapanthus, ageratum
it's Sunday evening, August
the locals have dressed up, showing off.
I listen to clicking heels, clink
of champagne glass, crunch of savoury
canapes and behind all that
the Baroque ensemble tuning up for
Monteverdi, Telemann, Bach.

Driving up the E52 from Munich
I avoided the road signposted
Concentration Camp Memorial.
Now I watch the animation on these faces
mostly young; that eases me, but some
old enough to have been in the story
fifty years ago when —

I know what ought to be said
but the narrative's tricky
I can't get the story-line
and it's not because my German's shaky.
In Masada and York the words come easy
in a language that slips off the tongue.
Perhaps in seven hundred years or so
I'll have learnt how to recite it.

Strange how we all sit close now
held by the music.

Looking for my Mother

Excuse me
I am looking for a young woman
somewhere in this area
in this street cul-de-sacked
by the dual carriage-way.
She may have knocked on this door
tapped on this window
beat the rhythm of these cobbles
with her pointed shoes.

Look, I've got all the photos
I know they're out of date.
Here she's in school uniform, black
and buttoned to the neck.
And this one's taken with my father.
She's got long hair —
you can see it glisten
even though the photo's gone brown.

She was over eighty when she died
but I'm looking for the young woman.
I'm sure her papers were in order
but she disappeared somewhere
between yesterday and today.

Hide and Seek

Ever since my mother died
she's played this game with me
and she always wins.
I hear her voice counting, counting
sometimes in the broom cupboard
sometimes when I'm chopping onions
I catch her eighteen, nineteen, twenty.
And then I hear her hissing
sixty-six, sixty-seven on the ironing board.
Then when she gets to ninety-nine
I put my hands over my eyes:
"You can't see me now," I shout.
But it's no use: "A hundred, coming!"
And I know she's found me.
"O.K., then," I say, "my turn now."
I count in tens to make it quick
but I never find her.
And it's her turn all over again.

Cote du Nacre

We copy Miss Cook's wobbly notes
in even wobblier French:
*"Ma Normandie, c'est le pays
qui m'a donne le jour."*

She reads us naughty novels:
the count who falls in love
with a boy dressed as a girl,
or is it a girl dressed as a boy?

We tingle as she ruffles the pages,
says, "We'd better skip this bit."
We sit on our hands, reach mentally
for something only half understood.

Now I'm on a Normandy beach shaped
by Miss Cook's wavering voice
light ebbing from the mother-of-pearl
sea, the mother-of-pearl sky.

I turn towards Ouistreham, its glitter
of seafood restaurants, the urgent
boom of the "Duc de Normandie"
taking tourists cross-channel.

Suddenly, I'm in a Polanski film
horses thundering along the sands
my camera's taking shots:
it's William, duke of Normandy

heading for the landing craft
away over to Hastings, London,
the motte and bailey castles
he'll build on every green hill

in England. Eat his fill of venison
captured from England's forests.
But this beach has a new name:
Sword Beach and I'm shooting

another film as horses' hooves fade
into 1944 gunfire: crowd scenes
courtesy of local villagers
battle scenes, D-Day Landings Ltd.

Part Two

WOMAN TAKING NOTES

1. Courier: Leningrad to Bialystok

Courier? Well, I had my arm twisted, didn't I?
Forward Tours? DIY Tours rather.
O.K. So I get the tour half price.
Twenty people and seventeen bunks and I
don't know a Polish fuck from a Russian arse.
Twenty, I say, holding up four hands:
two of my own, and two of this woman
standing next to me. The one who's always
making notes.
Then I go, "Bye, byes", lay my head on my hands,
take hers back and hold down three fingers.
Realise that leaves hers signing, "Up yours."
Whichever way, the Russian woman in charge
of bunks and samovars gets the message and
I get hers: "No bunk ticket, no bunk.
No bunk, no get on train."

Finally, the lost tickets turn up in
Liverpool Jim's pocket — he'd grabbed them
as souvenirs. So we're all set westwards
again. Long wait at the frontier to change
wheels and give Russian customs time to read
our leftover comics. Thank God for
Russian Rail's samovars at the end of every coach.
British Rail might take a hint or two.
That woman's noting it all down in her little book.

2. Jan at the Ghetto Memorial: Bialystok

There's a park just by our flats,
it's all right, mostly old men chatting
but when Mum's working at the clinic
there's nowhere much else to go.

Today this woman comes along.
older than Mum, more like Gran, really.
Stands by the memorial, reading all solemn
like she can't make out the words. Then
fiddles with her camera. I won't move,
just grin at her. She waves me aside,
then gives in and I'm in the photo too.
She points to the word: "Jews", then to herself.
So I goes, "I like Jews". I don't think
she understands, she must be foreign
or something. I try again:
"I like Jews," I go, "I don't like Germans."
Well, that's what Gran always says.
"Will you send me the photo?"
I write my address for her, though
I'm not right good at spelling.
Is it Protelarian or Proletarian Street?

Never mind. She searches her bag, gives
me two funny green stamps from England.
They've got a sideways lady with a crown
on her head all posh like. After that,
I take my new friend round our district,
show her the little wooden houses left
from years ago, not a bit like our flat.
I think I'd quite like to be a tour guide.

3. Headteacher, School No.XI: Bialystok

We're planning the new timetable
they've cut our budget again; the buildings —
two hundred years old some of them —
need repairing. Anna announces
a visitor, an English schoolteacher.
Thought she might have looked smarter.
She can't speak Polish and her Russian's
minimal. We talk ourselves back
eighty years through war, ghetto, war
and pogrom. There are old photos
girls in brown dresses and aprons
certificates for reciting Pushkin.
Tells me her mother went to Brussels
to study medicine but never qualified
got married instead. Well, it happens
now too though there is a Medical School
here in the Branicki Palace.

Says her school needs repairing, like ours.

4. The Archivist: Bialystok

You can only do half a job here:
no photocopier, no word processor.
Well, we know why and it's not only money.
So how can you research and record?
Like today, this woman comes in
tells me about her grandfather's factory.
I recognise the name. We trace it
in *The History of the Working Class,*
look through the index: strike after strike.
She tells me her father organised them.
That can't have pleased his old man.

There's no record of her mother's story:
once she took a message to workers in prison,
a note rolled inside a piece of bread
thrown over the railings.

We look at postcards, talk of Zamenhof.
I give her a book in Esperanto.
She promises to send me stuff from London.

5. American Tourist: Bialystok

We're having our breakfast
in the Lesny Hotel on the edge of town.
Not bad for Poland, summer 1987.
They've given us a little chalet in the woods.
The wife's people came from here,
that's why we've come back —
when this English woman rushes up
to us, all excited, flapping
the guide book. "Translate, this please!"
she says. Maria takes the book, smiles
at the English woman, reads:
*"Towards the end of the nineteenth century
the big Jewish textile firms included —"*
The woman grabs Maria's arm, points
to the names. "That's my grandfather."

Something stiffens inside me but I don't
say how Maria's grandfather emigrated
because he couldn't keep his family
on the wages paid by the Jewish
factory owners. Maria returns the book.
The woman goes, apparently satisfied.
We finish breakfast. I think
of our farm back in Wyoming.

6. Israeli Tourist: Bialystok

My daughter wouldn't come. You see,
we're on our way to our towns, our camps.
To come back is a kind of re-assurance
that we were here once and they know we were.
A facing of the past so that forgetting
can't turn into denial.

They were nice in my village,
knew my mother, said how she used to come
to the baker's every day. Showed me
the house I only half remember,
the one my daughter doesn't want to know.

Well, she's got the book of photos:
there's her granddad, the one who edited
a Zionist newspaper; and her grandmama,
strike leader in the cigarette factory.
That was before the first world war.
We don't know what happened to Aunt Esther.
Someone gave her a ticket to America;
she never got there. Very likely,
ended up in a brothel in Buenos Aires.
Better than a camp, perhaps.

We tell all this to the English woman.
She has the same stories for us.

7. Bus Driver: Bialystok to Zabludowa

You don't get many tourists on this route,
mostly locals shopping in town or going
to register, looking for work.
She pays, doesn't understand our money
as far as I can tell. Then looks
in her phrase book, tells me
her mother was born in Zabludowa before
the First World War. Doesn't look old
enough — dyes her hair, I shouldn't wonder.

There's a nice new town hall and co-op
I tell her but she doesn't seem to care.
Seems more interested in the old folk
with their horses and boat-shaped carts.
She's taking lots of photos of them.
Of course, she won't find the old wooden
synagogue with its upturned eaves like
something from China. Not that I ever
saw it. But my grandfather can remember
when Zabludowa was full of Jews. Like
they were all Jews in the street where
he lives now. Well, times change.

KEPLER'S WOMEN

1. Barbara Kepler writes to her husband, Johannes, in Graz Prague: 1601

I know thi, Johannes
Th'art in t' vineyard
wi' all t' green comin' through
an' I'm here at t' mercy of Tycho
I've nowt left, not a ha'p'orth of wood
an' tha talks about t' harmonies of heaven:
there's nowt as I can hear.
Will tha fetch me a new bodice,
mine is reet torn to shreds.
Me, I'd like a nice black one.
Eh, I nearly forgot to tell thi,
I took our Rogl to t'Emperor's garden
an flowers were bloomin' lovely.
Them lions roared fit to bust t' cages,
I were fair frit, an' our Rogl
she were howlin' like lions.
Have I to ask Tycho for money?
Tha never said we'd be clemmed to death
when tha wrote me horoscope.
Tha wain't forget t' bodice, will tha?
I know one thing for sure — there were
more money in one o' me father's vineyards
than in all thy stars put together.

2. Rogl, Kepler's stepdaughter, tells her story: 1603

I'm bringing him wine, white
and sweet, from our vineyards in Graz.
He sits there back to the window
his worn velvet catching the sun,
that same old sun that comes up
every day to warm us though he
says it's us as goes round the sun.
"Seeing is believing," I say but that's
not the truth of it, he says.
He's not my real Dad, see.
I like him well enough for all that,
short of money as we are.
I've not had a new skirt these last
five years, and I've grown that much
I'm bulging out of me old one.
But me, I'll not moither him.
He's at work on his optics now:
how the light gets into our eyes
and out again. Like I say
"Seeing is believing." Perhaps
one day he'll change his tune
and the Emperor'll pay his wages.
I put the jug on the red cloth
and the wine winks in the sun.
My shadow falls across his page.
He starts but his quill goes on
pecking and scratching the paper.
There's nowt'll stop him.

3. Susannah, Kepler's second wife, speaks: 1610

Tha chose me as never thought
to be thy wife. I were last
one seen out of the fourteen.
But me Nan saw me reet, told
thee all there were to know about me,
like I can sew fine and other things.
Them lazy lasses at Convent wasted
time and thread what wi' all the
knots they got into.
Me, I keep me threads short.
An' I'm reet good wi' bread.
I've a rare fist for dough,
rises lovely every time. I know well
how to tend herb garden. Me Nan
had rosemary, thyme an' a lot more.
They'll grow for me, I'll wager
though she never learnt me the recipes.
They tell me thy Mam is a fine brewer
of herbs. Maybe she'll learn me all I need.
I dunno as how I'll manage thy Rogl.
She's only a twelvemonth younger nor me.
But she'll help me wi' little 'uns,
I shouldn't wonder.

But will tha really love me?
An' shall I be able to love thee
as thy Barbara did all those years?
An' I've no letters like she had.
Shall I be wife or daughter?

4. Katharina Kepler to her son: Leonburg: August 1615

You must speak for me now that I am old.
You have studied the planets:
found out their secrets, the sweep of the line
from planet to sun, the harmonies of heaven.
But the world down here is strife-ridden.
Your father's off fighting in wars
that don't belong to any of us
and now they have taken my craft from me,
called me witch-woman, threatened my life.

When you were no more than a tiny lad
it was your mother showed you
the great comet trailing its tail
of fire above Ellmendingen; showed you how
to see the moon's eclipse through
a piece of smoked glass.
And when you lay in your cot burning
with fever it was the herbs I brewed
saved your life.

Leave your studies now, Johannes,
those wine barrels and their conic
sections. There's enough of a to-do
here in Leonburg to keep you busy.
I'll not tell you all they've said
it's been enough to frighten me:
that I've wished pains on the villagers,
maddened the neighbour's cattle,
ridden her calf to death. It's all
tittle-tattle set off by the mayor,
Luther Einhorn, and his cronies.
Your brothers are at their wits end.
Help me, Johannes.

THE TYRE-CAIRO LETTERS
Expanded from a fragment of parchment in the John Rylands Library, Manchester.

1. Sadaka to his father: Tyre October 1090

Father, they've given the post of cantor
to someone else —
do you remember the blue day of hope
I left Cairo with the oarsmen singing?
— to a pimply youth who intones without feeling
and an abominable accent.
Today is the first of Ramadan and the town
is on edge. The Jews keep close.
The streets are wet with the first
of the winter rains.
Give me your blessing. I am married now.
(You hoped Bathsheva Bat Eliahu
would be your new daughter.)
But give me your blessing even so.
It is Elisheva Bat Shmuel who has
found favour in my eyes.
Now the name of Sadaka Ha-Levi will
sound here in Tyre over the generations
when our sons and our sons' sons
are called in the synagogue.
I am in good health. I sing every day.
I send a son's love to my mother.
Sadaka Ha-Levi Ben Solomon.

2. Bathsheva to Sadaka Ha Levi: Cairo October 1090

Cairo is hot and I long for you.
Since you left I have done nothing
but weaving every day till my back aches,
My finger joints stiffen.
Today, my little brother pulled the threads
now they lie tangled on the floor tiles
making new patterns where the old are worn away.

I cannot sort out the wools:
Mother has cut the knotted lumps out
like some hideous growth
but the frayed ends hang forlorn.
She will beat Isaac for what he has done
but Father will praise him because he learns so well.
He will not see the red and blue bruises on Isaac's back.
Now I am sad.
I want my weaving ready for your return
but I do not know how to finish it.

3. The matchmaker to Sadaka's father:
Cairo December 1090

Honourable master, it is seven months now
since you visited me with your son
I found him an excellent match
a young girl well-provided for.
Her father's storehouse has silks and woollens,
you could not do better.
She is comely into the bargain:
her skin the colour of olives
her teeth white as a sheep's fleece
her eyes blue as the blown glass of Tyre.
Why has your son gone to that far off city
where the young girls are lewd and ugly?
The marriage has been arranged
and you must pay me the ten gold coins.
I am old now, I have waited too long:
my house needs a roof
before the winter rains destroy me.

4. Aviva Bat Solomon to her brother Sadaka:
Cairo December 1090

Distant brother, you say you are married now.
How I wish you could unsay those words.
Father has received your letter
but he will not reply
His wrath is the wrath of a jealous God:
the women of the family keep silent
while his anger roars through the house,
a hot wind in the season of the chamsin.
He walks the streets alone, his head to one side
unable to face Bathsheva's menfolk.

Your news is whispered from hearth to hearth
and the bales of wool that should have come
as Bathsheva's dowry gather dust in her father's shop.
Mother fears for Father's business
dreads that hunger will be the guest at our table.
I have no blessings to send you
only the wailings of a sad sister
who curses the white boat and those singing
oarsmen who rowed you to Tyre.

5. Elisheva Bat Shmuel to her mother-in-law: Tyre January 1091

Strange Mother, whom I have never met
I send you greeting from Tyre.
Now that I am one with your son
I shall love you as a dutiful daughter.
As the new moon pulls the tides of the sea
so each month my body will be prepared
and when my hopes are washed away
in that unclean flux
I shall be cleansed in the Mikvah
and my womb will be dedicated
to the grandchildren you desire.
Greet Ya'acov, the little brother whom I do not know
and kiss Aviva, my new sister
whom I long to meet.
How I envy the white birds who fly
to strange lands and new homes.
Though I cannot fly, my heart has wings.

6. Solomon to his son Sadaka: Cairo April 1091

Since you left, my fortunes have run dry
and I long for your return.
Today we have had the ceremony to mark
the rising of the Nile.
Kettledrums have sounded these three days,
trumpets have blasted our ears.
The stones of Cairo echo the hoofbeat
and march of the Caliph's army.
Men of wisdom have ridden with the princes
and your Uncle with the doctors of the court.
The Caliph dismounts at the head of the canal,
hurls his spade to make the first breach
and the slaves attack with pick and shovel:
the Nile floods.

The waters are blessed by the giving of alms
to the deaf-mutes in the first boat.
Now the markets of the city will swell
with the fruits of the earth,
but in my hearth there is an emptiness.

7. Bathsheba to Sadaka: Cairo July 1091

So you are married. I wish you well.
Now I am without the ties which held
me to you, I am a new person.
The days of weaving are gone, the lengths
of cloth which might have been my dowry
are sold and I am glad. Some other
woman can enjoy those coloured threads
which bound me for so many months.
I have opened a school. Women from Fustat
leave their blind teachers, come to our house.
I have collected flowers and herbs
and your uncle has named them for me.
Today I used tincture of iodine for a cut hand,
kaolin for a stomach that cannot keep its food.
I have begun to study the occulist's art.
Soon I shall see into the ways of men.

8. Sadaka to his father: Tyre April 1096

There is bad news from Constantinople:
They say the Franks are moving east
Travellers speak of massacres in Blois
a thousand Jews killed in Mainz.
The Franks want Jerusalem for their
three-in-one god and I fear for our safety.
The Caliph has increased our taxes
to pay for the defence of Tyre.
The town is full of snorting horses
and the flash of Muslim scimitars.
If you are willing to receive us in your house
we shall leave this threatened town
sail the blue road back to Cairo.
The curse of war will be lifted from us,
you will greet your granddaughters
and their shining faces will bless your old age.

9. Sarah to her son Sadaka: Cairo September 1096

My dearest son, your father is dead:
he died in the quiet of the night
in the new moon of Tishrei.
We have sat on low stools,
said Kaddish every day for seven days.
Now I must put aside my mourning:
there is work to be done.
Your sister Aviva has a good head for sums,
today she counted, sorted the bales.
I have employed three men from Fustat,
dyers who have brought their own vats,
installed them in the outside sheds.
The wood is rotten and I fear we shall have
dye leaking into the courtyard.
Worse still, Ya'acov spends his time
with these men when he should be learning.
There is no-one to tell him — if only your father —
but such thoughts are useless:
dyed cloth makes a good profit.

10. Elisheva Bat Shmuel to her sister-in-law: Tyre December 1096

Sister, Aviva, I write to you
though we know each other only by name.
One woe follows on the heels of another.
Sadaka is dead.
The Franks fired the synagogue in Antioch:
he had gone there to sing Kaddish. The rabbis
tell us we should not grieve:
the dead have found a safe harbour
but his was too short a journey.
Now I shelter with the widow, Leah
but fear of the Franks is all around us.
I do not know how long Tyre will be safe.
Leah has ships bound for Cairo
with cargoes of tabby carpets
rose and violet-water in Tyre glass.
We will cross the sea that brought Sadaka here.
You will have a new sister to help
with the dyestuffs and your mother a new daughter.
As women we shall be strong, give each other comfort
and my daughters will grow in a place of peace.

Glossary

Cantor — leader of singing and prayers in the synagogue.

Challah — braided bread, traditionally eaten at the Friday evening (Sabbath) meal.

Chanucah — Jewish festival of lights, held in December.

Gimel — Hebrew letter pronounced "g".

Hamantaschen — three-cornered poppy-seed cake eaten at Purim, representing Haman's hat.

Kaddish — prayer for the dead.

Kiddush — blessing over wine and bread on the Sabbath and at festivals.

Mandate — the period of British control over Palestine.

Ma nish-tanah ha lie-lah ha-zay? — The first of the four questions asked by the youngest at the Passover meal. "Why is this night different from all others?"

Ma-oz-tzur ye shou-a-ti... — the opening words of one of the Chanucah songs.

Mikvah — ritual bath.

Passover — festival celebrating the escape of Jews from slavery in Egypt.

Purim — celebration of Esther foiling Haman's plot against Jews, traditionally involving fancy dress.

Samech, vav, samech — Hebrew letters spelling "soos", horse.

Shamash — The "servant" candle, which lights all the others on the Chanucah candelabra.

Spiel — story.

Schwester — sister.

Tishrei — the month in which the Jewish New Year falls.

Zamenhof — the inventor of Esperanto.

Bialystok, from where Liz Cashdan's family originated, and which provides the setting for many of these poems is a Polish town, previously under Russian control. Prior to World War Two Jews made up half the population of 80,000. Bialystok was a major centre for textiles and for Jewish labour union activity.

Also Available From Five Leaves Publications

- **THE DYBBUK OF DELIGHT: AN ANTHOLOGY OF JEWISH WOMEN'S POETRY**
Edited by Sonja Lyndon and Sylvia Paskin
Paperback, 192 pages, £8.99.
0 907123 56 2

> *"I am the dybbuk of delight*
> *I slip into the souls of those who need me"*
> Michelene Wandor

A major celebration of contemporary Jewish women's poetry — contributors include Michelene Wandor, Elaine Feinstein, Ruth Fainlight, Lotte Kramer and many more.

Published 11/95

- **YOU ARE, AREN'T YOU?**
Michael Rosen
Paperback, 72 pages, £4.99.
0 907123 09 0

Bringing together Michael Rosen's Jewish poetry, this collection shows the author's unique wit and observation, and his anger at injustice and hypocrisy.

Further copies of *Laughing All the Way* and the above titles can be ordered through bookshops or purchased post-free from Five Leaves Publications, PO Box 81, Nottingham NG5 4ER.